W9-BUX-734

Dear Parent:
Your child's love of reading starts here!

Every child learns to read in a different way and at his or her own speed. Some go back and forth between reading levels and read favorite books again and again. Others read through each level in order. You can help your young reader improve and become more confident by encouraging his or her own interests and abilities. From books your child reads with you to the first books he or she reads alone, there are I Can Read Books for every stage of reading:

SHARED READING
Basic language, word repetition, and whimsical illustrations, ideal for sharing with your emergent reader

BEGINNING READING
Short sentences, familiar words, and simple concepts for children eager to read on their own

READING WITH HELP
Engaging stories, longer sentences, and language play for developing readers

READING ALONE
Complex plots, challenging vocabulary, and high-interest topics for the independent reader

ADVANCED READING
Short paragraphs, chapters, and exciting themes for the perfect bridge to chapter books

I Can Read Books have introduced children to the joy of reading since 1957. Featuring award-winning authors and illustrators and a fabulous cast of beloved characters, I Can Read Books set the standard for beginning readers.

A lifetime of discovery begins with the magical words "I Can Read!"

Visit www.icanread.com for information
on enriching your child's reading experience.

I Can Read Book® is a trademark of HarperCollins Publishers.

Library of Congress catalog card number: 2011938182
ISBN 978-0-06-195821-2 (trade bdg.) — ISBN 978-0-06-195820-5 (pbk.)

12 13 14 15 16   SCP   10 9 8 7 6 5 4 3 2 1   ❖   First Edition

I Can Read!™ SHARED My First READING

everything GOES

HENRY GOES SKATING

Based on the Everything Goes books
by BRIAN BIGGS

Illustrations in the style of Brian Biggs
by SIMON ABBOTT

Text by B.B. BOURNE

HARPER
An Imprint of HarperCollinsPublishers

Henry wakes up.

He looks out the window.

"Snow!" Henry says.

"I can make a snowman."

"Who wants to go skating?"
asks Mom.

"I do!" Henry says.

"I want to go skating."

Henry is in the car.

He sees a snowplow.

Henry sees a dump truck.

He sees a bus.

Uh-oh!

The bus is stuck.

It cannot go on the ice.

A tow truck comes.

The tow truck tows the bus.

The bus is off the ice.

Now the bus can go.

More snow falls.

"Go slow, Dad," Henry says.
"We don't want to get stuck."
"I will go slow," says Dad.

Henry sees the park.

The trees are white.

Yellow taxis pass by.

A dog pulls a sled.

"What fun!" Henry says.

"Woof!" the dog says.

"Look, Henry. Horses!"
says Henry's mom.

"Police horses," says Henry.
"One is brown and one is white.
And one is brown and white."

"Buses get stuck," Henry says.
"Even trucks get stuck.
But horses can go in the snow."

"We're here," says Henry.
Dad parks the car.

Henry puts on his skates.
Dad helps.

Henry goes to the ice.

No one is skating.

Everyone looks at the ice.

Henry stands on a bench.

"It's a Zamboni!" he says.

"It will smooth the ice."

The Zamboni goes up.

The Zamboni goes down.

The Zamboni goes around.

Now everyone can skate!

"Look!" Henry says.

"I can go up.

I can go down.

I can go around
and around."

28

"Like a Zamboni," Dad says.

Henry skates and skates.

At last it is time to go home.
"That was fun," Henry says.

Henry looks out the window.

He sees snow on the cars.

He sees snow on the road.

"We're home," Henry says.
"Time to make a snowman!"